Nothing Ever Happens at the South Pole

Stan & Jan
Berenstain

HARPER

An Imprint of HarperCollinsPublishers

Nothing Ever Happens at the South Pole
Copyright © 2012 by Berenstain Enterprises, Inc.
All rights reserved. Manufactured in China.
No part of this book may be used or reproduced in any manner whatsoever without written
permission except in the case of brief quotations embodied in critical articles and reviews.
For information address HarperCollins Children's Books, a division of HarperCollins Publishers,
10 East 53rd Street, New York, NY 10022.
www.harpercollinschildrens.com

Library of Congress Cataloging-in-Publication Data is available.
ISBN 978-0-06-207532-1

Typography by Tom Starace
12 13 14 15 16   SCP   10 9 8 7 6 5 4 3 2 1
❖
First Edition

Oh, boy! The mail!
The mail has come!
There is mail today,
and I got some!

It is a book!
A book for me!
A book to write in—
now, that's for me!

I cannot wait
to start my book.
Something might happen.
All I have to do is look.

It does not matter
which way I go.
Something is sure to happen
in all this snow.

Hey! Something happened!
I made a snowball! Look!
I can write that down
in my book!

No! That is no good—
I made a snowball. Look.
That is not good
for my new book!

A giant snowball
would be good.
That I could write about—
yes, I could.
A snowball that
went round and round
and smashed some baddies
to the ground.

But that snow back there
was much too thin
for anything good
to happen in.

This snow is thick
and full of lumps.
Lumps like these
would make good jumps!

One, two, three, four—
this is really great!
I'll keep jumping—
five, six, seven, eight—

until I've jumped
a hundred jumps
from lump to lump
on all these humps.

I'll write that down.
It will say—
I jumped a hundred
jumps today!

No. I jumped a hundred
jumps today
is not a good enough
thing to say.

It might be good
if they were jumps
on some big monsters
with lumpy humps!

Some big monsters
got in a fight
and rolled around
from day to night.

That is something
I would like to write.
Something like that
would be great, all right!

But nothing will happen
back there today.
Too many lumps
are in the way.

Now, here is really
something to see—
stepping-stones made
of ice for me!

A little step here,
a giant step there—
it may be dangerous,
but I don't care!

I'll put that down!
I'll write and say—
I did a dangerous
thing today!

Not bad! Not bad!
It is the best yet.
How much more dangerous
can you get?

No. That was not
dangerous enough.
There should be something
BIG and TOUGH!

Something big
and something tough
might do something
BIG and ROUGH!

Yes, that's it!
I'll look and see
where something really
BIG might be.

Something big
will happen now
when I punch that
big thing's eye—POW!

That was no eye
for me to sock.
It was just a snail
on a hunk of rock.

This place is nothing
but rocks and snails
that look like
great big eyes of whales.

If a whale that big
had an eye that high
he wouldn't ever
let me by.

He would open his mouth
like a giant cave
and swallow me down
like a giant wave.

A thing like that
would be great to read,
but a thing like that
I do not need!

I must write SOMETHING!
It is almost night.
There is just one thing
for me to write.

It is the only thing
I CAN say—

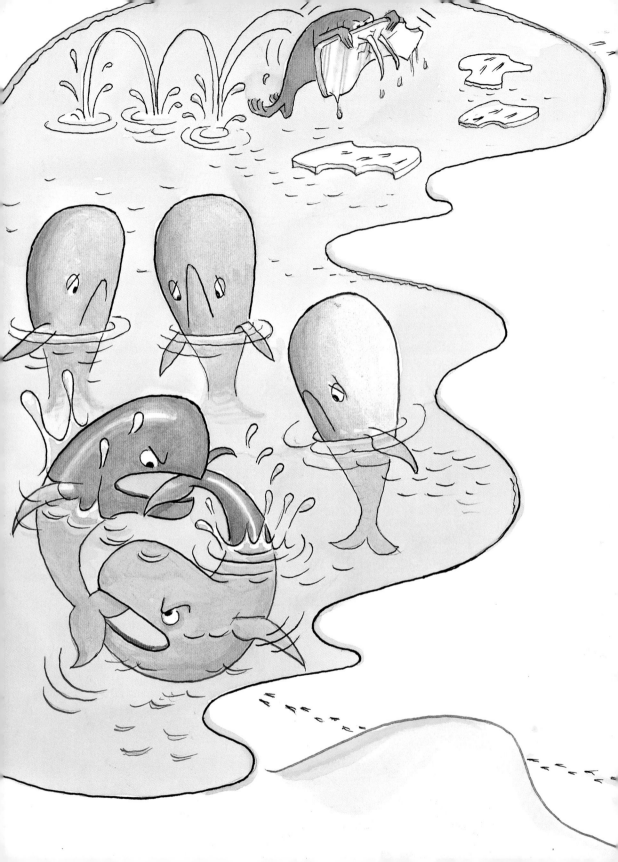

Nothing ever happens at the
South Pole—

But I will look again tomorrow, anyway!